An I Can Read Book®

Chang's Paper Pony

by Eleanor Coerr

Pictures
by Deborah Kogan Ray

Harper & Row, Publishers

Chang's Paper Pony
Text copyright © 1988 by Eleanor Coerr
Illustrations copyright © 1988 by Deborah Kogan
All rights reserved. No part of this book may be
used or reproduced in any manner whatsoever without
written permission except in the case of brief quotations
embodied in critical articles and reviews. Printed in
the United States of America. For information address
Harper & Row Junior Books, 10 East 53rd Street,
New York, N.Y. 10022. Published simultaneously in
Canada by Fitzhenry & Whiteside Limited, Toronto.
1   2   3   4   5   6   7   8   9   10
First Edition

Library of Congress Cataloging-in-Publication Data
Coerr, Eleanor.
    Chang's paper pony.

    (An I can read book)
    Summary: In San Francisco during the 1850's gold
rush, Chang, the son of Chinese immigrants, wants a
pony but cannot afford one until his friend Big Pete
finds a solution.
    [1. Chinese Americans—Fiction.   2. Ponies—Fiction.
3. Gold mines and mining—Fiction]   I. Kogan, Deborah,
ill.   II. Title.   III. Series.
PZ7.C6567Ch   1988   [E]   87-45679
ISBN 0-06-021328-0
ISBN 0-06-021329-9 (lib. bdg.)

To the Chinese in California

CONTENTS

CHANG'S WISH

Chang and Grandpa Li

were peeling potatoes in the kitchen

of the Gold Ditch Hotel.

Suddenly Chang stopped.

"I hear horses!" he cried,

and ran to the door.

"If only I had a pony,"

he told Grandpa Li,

"I would never be lonely."

"Next year," said Grandpa Li,

"the miners will bring their families,"

"You will not be lonely then."

But Chang was not sure.

He remembered the day

he and Grandpa Li had arrived

in San Francisco.

He remembered how some boys

had thrown stones at them.

"American children hate us,"

Chang said.

Grandpa Li shook his head.

"They do not hate us," he said.

"They just do not understand us."

"I would rather have a pony.

Then I would really have a *pengyo*—

a friend," Chang said.

Grandpa Li smiled.

"You have friends now," he said.

"There is your teacher,

and the barber,

and the blacksmith.

And don't forget Big Pete."

"They are too old to play with,"

Chang said.

"But I could play with a pony."

Grandpa Li pointed to a painting
tacked above the stove.
"That is the only pony
we can afford," he said.
"Now finish peeling the potatoes.
Hungry miners will soon come
for my good supper."

Chang did as he was told.

He also set the tables,

brought water from the well,

and carried in wood for the stove.

13

All the time

he wished he had a pony.

TROUBLE

Some miners were rough.

They liked to yank Chang's pigtail.

Chang tried to keep his pigtail

out of their reach.

And he was always polite.

When a miner asked him his name,

Chang bowed low and said,

"My humble name is Chang."

The miner slapped his knee.

"Doesn't that pop your eyeballs!"

he cried.

Everyone laughed.

Chang ran into the kitchen.

"I want to go home to China,"
he said.

Grandpa Li held him close.

"You know we can't go back,"

he said.

"There is a war in China."

"But those miners—

why are they so mean?"

asked Chang.

Grandpa Li sighed.

"They left their hearts at home,"

he said.

"All they can think about is gold.

And gold fever

makes them a little crazy."

After supper Chang took a bath
in the big tub.
Then he tightened his pigtail
and put on clean clothes.

He walked down the dusty main street

to his lessons.

Chang stopped to look

at the horses in the town stable.

"When I have a pony," he thought,

"I will keep him here."

Scholar See Yow taught Chang
to read and write English.
How Chang hated it!
The words looked like ugly worms
wiggling across the paper.

tsu—child

 jen—man

 shan—mountain

 ma—horse

Chang liked painting Chinese words
with a pointed brush and black ink.
Each word looked like a picture:
tsu—child, *jen*—man, *shan*—mountain.
When he came to *ma*—horse,
Chang began to daydream.

23

CRAAAAACK!

Scholar See Yow's stick came down

across Chang's skinny back.

"If you don't stop playing,"

the teacher said,

"you will be an empty bamboo—

good for nothing."

Chang swallowed hard.

He did not care

about being an empty bamboo.

All he wanted was a pony.

That night Chang hugged his pillow.

He pretended it was his pony's neck.

He could almost feel its soft nose

and hear it breathing.

BIG PETE

Things got better for Chang

when Big Pete came to Gold Ditch.

Big Pete was the tallest,

strongest man

Chang had ever seen.

He never pulled Chang's pigtail

or teased him.

It was getting very busy
in Gold Ditch.

28

More and more miners came
every day.

They dug for gold

in the mountains.

They panned for gold

in the rivers.

They weighed their gold nuggets

on Big Pete's scales.

Tiny flakes of gold

fell to the floor.

The men only cared

about big nuggets of gold.

One day Big Pete showed Chang
some of the big nuggets.

That was when Chang got an idea.

"Big Pete, will you show me

how to look for gold?" he asked.

"I need gold to buy a pony."

Big Pete looked at Chang.

"A pony costs a heap of money," he said.

"Please," said Chang.

"I will clean your cabin

and scrub your floor."

Big Pete laughed.

"Tell you what," he said.

"If your grandpa says okay,

I will take you tomorrow."

Chang gave a shout

and ran to the Gold Ditch Hotel.

"Please, please let me go,"

he begged.

"Ahummmmmm," said Grandpa Li.

Chang held his breath and waited.

Finally, Grandpa nodded.

"Just this once," he said.

"Maybe the fat God of Luck

will smile upon you."

GOLD FEVER

Early the next morning

Grandpa Li packed a lunch

for Chang and Big Pete.

Chang took a bag

to put the gold in.

Big Pete lifted him onto his horse.

"HY-AAAAAH!" he yelled,

and they rode off.

At a deep ditch

Big Pete handed Chang

a shovel and pail.

The ground was like rock.

40

Big Pete loosened it with a pick.

Chang scooped up the earth

with his shovel.

41

Big Pete showed Chang

how to pan for gold in the river.

He poured some earth into a pan.

Then he rocked and twisted it

in the water.

When the mud washed away,

there were sand and pebbles.

But not a speck of gold.

Chang worked hard.

The sun grew hot.

Sweat ran down his face,

and his hands got blistered.

"Go easy, pardner,"

said Big Pete.

"The gold will not run away."

But Chang could not slow down.

He wanted his pony!

Suddenly, Chang let out a shout.

"YOWEEE! GOLD!"

Flakes of gold

glittered among the pebbles and sand

in his pan.

Chang carefully poured it all

into his bag.

He and Big Pete

galloped into Gold Ditch.

"Now I can have my pony!"

Chang shouted.

Chang spread the treasure

on the kitchen table.

Big Pete helped him blow away

all the sand and dirt.

Chang stared at what was left.

"That will not even buy a goat,"

he said sadly.

"Now I will never have a pony."

THE REAL PONY

In the morning

Chang kept his promise.

He took a broom to Big Pete's cabin

and began to sweep.

Suddenly he saw something glittering
between the wooden boards.

Chang knelt down for a closer look.
"Gold!" he whispered.

The pieces were no bigger

than a pinhead,

but there were lots of them.

Maybe enough to buy a pony!

He put all the gold flakes into a pail

and ran home to show Grandpa Li.

"Now I can buy a pony, for sure!"

Chang cried.

Grandpa Li gave Chang

a long, hard look.

"Of course you will give the gold

to Big Pete," he said.

"It was in his cabin."

"I...I guess so," said Chang.

His dream of having a pony

faded away.

"By jingo!" Big Pete said.
"I never knew there was
so much gold in my floor."

Big Pete took the gold
to the bank in Sacramento.

Chang took down the paper pony
and tried to forget his dream.

One afternoon Chang heard

a clippity-clop.

"That's Big Pete's horse,"

said Grandpa Li.

"I know," said Chang.

Slowly, he walked to the door.

There was Big Pete.

He was leading a handsome pony.

"He is all yours, pardner," Big Pete said.

"I bought him

with your share of the gold."

Chang gently reached out

and rubbed the pony's moist nose.

The pony nuzzled Chang's fingers

and whinnied softly.

A big smile spread

across Chang's face.

"I think he likes me," he said.

Big Pete swung Chang up
onto the pony's back.

Chang felt he would burst for joy.

"My own pony!" he cried.

"I will call you Pengyo."

Chang leaned over and whispered

into the pony's ear,

"I love you, Pengyo."

Pengyo gave a little snort,

as if he understood.

Wars and revolutions throughout China
caused thousands of Chinese to come to
America between 1850 and 1864. Many
came to seek their fortunes in "Gold Mountain," the name they gave to California.
Some were carpenters, farmers, engineers,
scholars, and doctors. Others helped build
the first transcontinental railroad. The Chinese had no legal rights in this country and
were sometimes treated cruelly.

American miners, like Big Pete, often left
gold dust on the floor. The Chinese workers
who cleaned their cabins gladly swept up the
gold dust for themselves.

Although the Chinese contributed much
to our country, especially in California, few
of those early immigrants made the fortunes
they came to find.

64